HARDCOURT COMEBACK

FRED BOWEN

PEACHTREE
ATLANTA

Published by
PEACHTREE PUBLISHERS
1700 Chattahoochee Avenue
Atlanta, Georgia 30318-2112
www.peachtree-online.com

Text © 2010 by Fred Bowen

Printed and bound in the United States of America by RR Donnelley in Harrisonburg, Virginia
10 9 8 7 6 5 4 3 2 1
First Edition

Library of Congress Cataloging-in-Publication Data
    Bowen, Fred.
        Hardcourt comeback / written by Fred Bowen.
            p. cm.
        Summary: Seventh-grade basketball star Brett is used to being good, if not the best, at everything he does, but after finding one thing he cannot do he loses confidence and starts making mistakes.
        ISBN: 978-1-56145-516-4
        [1. Basketball--Fiction. 2. Self-confidence--Fiction.] I. Title.
        PZ7.B6724Har 2010
        [Fic]--dc22

For Valerie Tripp:
Writing friend, family friend, my friend

Layup drill!" Coach Giminski shouted above the sounds of pounding basketballs. The Wildcats, a team of seventh graders in the Rising Stars League, snapped into action, moving swiftly to fill the shooting, rebounding, and passing lines. "Count 'em off," the coach ordered.

Brett Carter, the Wildcats star forward, caught a bounce pass from Will Giminski, his teammate and best friend. Brett took a quick, confident dribble to the basket. He pushed off with his left foot and laid the ball against the top right corner of the square outlined on the glass backboard. The ball dropped through the net. *Swish*.

"One," Brett called. He circled under the basket to the back of the rebounding line.

Each player shouted out a number as the ball went into the basket.

"Two..."

"Three..."

"Four..."

"Make 'em all," the coach instructed. "Remember, you guys can't scrimmage until you make twenty in a row."

"Five..."

"Six..."

"Seven..."

On the eighth attempt, Antwon Davis, a reserve guard, put the ball up too hard against the backboard. It bounced off the front of the rim and fell away. The Wildcats groaned.

"Come on, Antwon," Brett barked. "Concentrate. We gotta make twenty."

"Start it over," Coach Giminski called.

The count began again as the coach watched from the sidelines, a silver whistle dangling from his neck. "Come on, the layup is the easiest shot in basketball," he said. "Use the backboard. Take it strong to the hoop."

The count was at sixteen when Brett bounced a perfect waist-high pass to Will. But his friend fumbled the ball and it slipped out of bounds.

"Start it again!" his father demanded.

Brett and Will stood in the rebounding line together. "Choker," Brett teased.

"Give me a break," Will muttered. "It slipped."

"You choked," Brett insisted.

"Just make *your* shots, okay?" Will snapped.

The count gradually got closer and closer to the magic number: seventeen...eighteen...nineteen....

Antwon tossed a pass to Brett. Without hesitation, Brett dribbled hard to the basket, laid the ball against the backboard, and watched the ball fall through the net.

"That's twenty!" he shouted. He turned toward his cheering teammates and pumped his fist into the air.

The coach blew his whistle. "All right, scrimmage time," he said.

Seconds later, the Wildcats cheered even

louder as Coach Giminski began to divide the squad. "Okay, let's have Brett be captain of one team and Will captain of the other."

Brett and Will stood across from each other at midcourt. As the Wildcats starting forwards and best players, Brett and Will were always the captains in scrimmages. They were both tall and athletic. With their dark hair, they could have been mistaken for brothers. But though they were close in ability, Brett was always a bit quicker and better than Will.

"Jeremy Sims, Robert Maldonado, Christian Reyes, and Antwon Davis, you're on Will's team," Coach Giminski said. "Ellis Lee, Gabriel Matos, Troy Jensen, and Garrett Fox, you're with Brett."

"Hey, Dad, what defense do you want us to play?" Will asked.

"Man-to-man," Coach Giminski said. He bounced the ball to Garrett to start the game. "First team to ten baskets wins. I want to see lots of passes and picks out there."

Brett and Will ran upcourt side by side.

"Ready to lose again?" Brett kidded his friend.

"What are you talking about?" Will said as he began to play defense against Brett. "We've got Jeremy. He can score."

Brett's team jumped off to a quick lead as Brett canned two jump shots. "So when are you guys going to start playing?" Brett said as he backpedaled downcourt after the second basket.

Will charged by Brett for a quick layup. Then Jeremy, the Wildcats starting center, tapped an offensive rebound back to the basket. A minute later he tapped back another rebound. *Swish* again!

Now it was Will's turn for a little trash talk. "You guys taking a rest on defense, or what?"

Brett answered by hitting a jump shot from the corner to tie the score, 3–3. "What did you say, Will?" he said, still needling his friend.

"Don't let him have that shot," Coach Giminski warned his son. "Go out and cover him."

Will got the ball on the right wing, but Brett kept up his chatter even while playing defense. "Listen to your old man, Will," he said. "Better not let me have that shot."

The game went back and forth. Neither team was able to get more than a basket ahead. All the Wildcats were playing hard. Everyone wanted the bragging rights of a win against their teammates. Finally Will hit a turnaround jump shot, even with Brett draped all over him. The game was tied at 9–9.

"You'd better not let me have *that* shot," Will told Brett as they ran upcourt.

"Next basket wins," Coach Giminski called.

Brett ran down the right side of the court with Will trailing close beside him. He leaned to the left and started heading to the other side of the court. His friend stayed close. When Brett suddenly stopped and pivoted to the right, Will kept going, then turned and ran toward Brett.

Garrett was bringing the ball up, saw the move, and hit Brett with a pass about

20 feet from the basket. Brett caught it and pumped the ball high as if he were going to shoot. Will leaped to block the shot. As Will flew through the air, Brett pulled the ball down and dribbled past him, threading his way to the basket. With one final step, Brett angled by Jeremy and laid the ball against the backboard. The ball splashed through the net.

Brett's team had won, 10–9!

Tweeeet! the coach's whistle shrieked. "Okay, that's it. Practice is over," he called. "Clear out, guys."

The Wildcats gathered their gym bags and water bottles scattered along the gymnasium walls.

"Nice layup," Brett's twin sister Brooke said. She was standing on the sideline with a basketball under her arm, waiting to practice with her own team.

Brett grinned. "Yeah. I faked Will out of his shoes."

"He'll be steamed about that," Brooke said.

"I know." Brett took a long gulp of water. "Is Dad here yet?"

"He said he's running late. He'll be here in about an hour."

"That's okay, I've got a book," Brett said. "Hey, how's your team looking so far?"

"Real good," Brooke said. "We've got the Carlson sisters, Sonja and Renee. They can score."

"And they've got you," Brett reminded his sister. "You're good."

Brooke shrugged. "We'll be okay."

Coach Giminski and Will walked by them on their way out of the gym. "Nice fake," Coach Giminski said to Brett. "Always be thinking about getting to the basket. Like I said, layups are the easiest shots in basketball."

Brett nodded and eyed Will. His friend didn't look happy.

"And you," Coach Giminski said, playfully nudging his son in the ribs. "I've told you a million times, stay on your feet on defense. You can't cover anybody flying through the air."

"I know, I know." Will rolled his eyes.

After the Giminskis had left, Brett sat

down in the corner of the gym. The smooth, hard wall felt cool on the back of his sweaty T-shirt. He pulled his book out of his backpack. Then he looked out on the court. Brooke, the Carlsons, and the rest of the team were warming up by shooting layups. Brett rested his head against the wall, thought of his own game-winning layup, and smiled.

Chapter 2

"We're home!" Mr. Carter called as he entered the house with Brett and Brooke. In the corner of the living room, Jumper, the family's West Highland terrier, stirred on his pillow and fell back to sleep.

"I'll be down in a second," Mrs. Carter replied from upstairs. "I'm on the phone with Grandma."

Brett grabbed a glass from the cupboard. He walked over to the refrigerator, pushed a button, and filled the glass with cold, filtered water. He gulped greedily as he stared at the two report cards posted side by side on the refrigerator.

Brooke Carter		Brett Carter	
English	A	English	A
Math	A	Math	A
Social Studies	A	Social Studies	B
Science	A	Science	A
French	A	Spanish	A
Physical Educ.	A	Physical Educ.	A

"Looking at that B in social studies isn't going to change it to an A," Brooke teased as she filled her glass with water.

"If I get an A this quarter, I'll get an A for the semester," Brett said. "Then we'll be tied."

"Maybe you'll win the social studies bee next week," Brooke said. "It counts toward our early American history unit."

"Want to help me study?" Brett asked.

"What about me?" Brooke asked. "I want to win too, you know."

"I need more help than you," Brett said. "I'm the guy who got the B, remember?"

Brooke smiled but didn't say anything.

"Come on," Brett pleaded. "I'll ask you some questions too."

"Okay," she said.

"Do you two have much homework?" Mr. Carter asked from the dining room as he looked through the day's mail.

"Not much," Brett answered. "Just studying for the history bee next week."

Mrs. Carter came downstairs and gave her husband a kiss on the cheek.

"How's your mom?" he asked.

"Fine," she answered and then turned to Brooke. "She may come to your game on Sunday."

"Hey, what about my game?" Brett asked, pretending to be insulted.

"I'm sure Grandma will make it to one of yours this season too. Don't worry," Mrs. Carter said. "How was practice?"

"Great," Brett and Brooke answered at the same time.

"I scored the winning basket in our scrimmage," Brett boasted. "I faked Will out big-time. He was pretty annoyed."

"I hope you didn't give him a hard time about it," Brett's mother said, frowning.

"Huh? Well, maybe a little," Brett admitted. "But I was just joking. We're still best buds."

"You two better get started on your homework," Mrs. Carter said.

Brett and Brooke scrambled up the stairs to their rooms. Brett tossed his backpack on his unmade bed. As he changed his clothes, he looked around the crowded bedroom. The walls were covered with sports posters, as well as tickets and programs from games he had attended. In the corner of the room, the top of his dresser was filled with trophies from his soccer, basketball, and baseball teams. Beside the dresser, next to a heap of dirty clothes, was a stack of old sports magazines. Brett walked over to his cluttered desk to study the Wildcats schedule.

RISING STARS LEAGUE—BIG EAST CONFERENCE

Date	Opponent	Time	
Dec. 13	Panthers	1 p.m.	W 41-36
Dec. 20	Golden Eagles	2 p.m.	W 50-26
Jan. 10	Orangemen	4 p. m.	W 38-29
Jan. 17	Cardinals	noon	W 49-40
Jan. 24	Panthers	3 p.m.	
Jan. 31	Huskies	2 p.m.	
Feb. 7	Orangemen	1 p.m.	
Feb. 14	Golden Eagles	4 p.m.	
Feb. 21	Cardinals	noon	
Feb. 28	Huskies	1 p.m.	

We better beat the Panthers on Sunday, he thought, *because the Huskies are going to be really tough.* Then he grabbed a notebook and headed to his sister's room across the hall.

"Come in," Brooke said after Brett knocked on the door. She was at her computer, typing out a message. Her room was a lot neater than Brett's. The light green walls were covered with posters of her favorite actors, actresses, and rock bands. Her clothes were neatly put away in her dresser. But the top, just like Brett's, was covered with trophies.

"Want to quiz me on the history stuff now?" Brett asked.

"Okay."

Brett handed his sister the notebook. He flopped on her bed and grabbed a pillow for his head. "Start with the last section," he instructed. "You know, the one on the Civil War. I know the stuff before that pretty well."

Brooke studied the paper. "Okay," she began. "Try this one. Who was the president of the Confederacy?"

"That's easy." Brett smiled. "Jefferson Davis."

The questions and answers went back and forth like passes in a layup drill.

"What did President Lincoln issue on January 1, 1863?"

"The Emancipation Proclamation."

"What did the Emancipation Proclamation do?"

"It freed the slaves."

"Who was the general for the Confederates at the Battle of Gettysburg?"

"Robert E. Lee."

"Who was the Union general?"

"Meade."

Brooke raised her eyebrows.

"Okay, okay. George Gordon Meade," Brett said.

"These are too easy. I'm going to find a really tough one." Brooke glanced down the page. "Okay, here's one you'll never get."

"On the third day of the Battle of Gettysburg, one of the Confederate generals led a famous charge. Who was it?"

"I know this. I know this...." Brett pounded his forehead, trying to knock the answer loose.

"That won't help," his sister told him.

"Give me a hint," Brett pleaded.

"No way," Brooke said. "Mr. McMillan and Ms. Fromm won't give you any hints."

"Come on, just one."

"Okay." Brooke thought for a moment. "What do you do with your nose all the time?"

"What?" Brett said. Then he had the answer. "Pick it!" he blurted out. "General George E. Pickett."

"Right." Brooke laughed.

Brett punched the air as if he had scored a winning basket.

Chapter 3

"Concentrate, now," Coach Giminski said as the Wildcats shot layups before the Panthers game. "I want you to make every shot."

Will laid one up and in, followed quickly by Brett. The coach stood on the sidelines with his hands on his hips. "Take it up strong. No fancy stuff," he said. "Easiest shot in basketball."

After a few more layups, he called out, "Okay, let's bring it in."

The Wildcats gathered around in a tight circle. Brett saw his sister sitting on the Wildcats bench, keeping the scorebook for Coach Giminski. Her team had won earlier in the day.

The coach went through his usual last-minute reminders to hustle, play defense, and move the ball on offense. Then he motioned to Brooke to hand him the score-book. "Okay, here's the starting lineup," he said. "Jeremy's at center. Brett and Will are starting at forwards. Garrett and Christian are in the backcourt. Everybody's going to get in today, so pay attention on the bench." He put his hand into the middle of the circle. All the Wildcats piled their hands on top of his.

"One...two...three...defense!" they shouted.

The game started slowly with both teams playing tight man-to-man defense. After more than two minutes, with the score tied 0–0, Brett got the ball near the left side of the foul line. A Panthers defender was all over him, but quick-thinking Will rushed over and set a pick to Brett's right. Brett faked left and went right around Will, who blocked the defender's path. Brett dribbled free toward the basket and shot a twisting layup just as the Panthers center bumped him off balance. The ball bounced around the rim and fell in as the referee's whistle blew.

"The basket is good!" the referee shouted, motioning with his hand, "Foul on Number 10. One shot."

Brett traded high fives with his teammates. Then he stepped to the line and confidently sank the free throw. The Wildcats now led 3–0.

Brett's basket seemed to wake up both teams. The score mounted higher as the Wildcats and the Panthers traded baskets. At the end of the quarter, Brett's three-point play was still the difference as the Wildcats led 11–8.

Early in the second quarter, Brett and Will sat on the bench, gulping water and watching the Wildcats reserves play. "Hey," Brett said, "when we go back in, let's try that same play where you set a pick for me, okay?" His friend nodded. "But if they move over to cover me," Brett added, "I'll flip it back to you for a quick jumper. You should be wide open." The two of them tapped fists and looked back at the court.

The Panthers scored several quick baskets to grab the lead, 16–15. "Brett. Will," Coach Giminski said, snapping his fingers. "Get in there for Ellis and Robert."

Back in the game, Brett and Will worked their plan. Brett got the ball on the left wing and Will set a pick near the foul line. Just like before, Brett drove hard around Will, who blocked the defender. But this time, other defenders were ready and tried to cut off Brett's path to the basket. Brett leaped in the air, spun, and flipped a pass back to Will, who shot a picture-perfect jump shot.

Swish!

"Yes!" Brett shouted.

Two more baskets by Brett, one on a jump shot and another on a drive to the basket, helped the Wildcats hold on to a slim 21–20 lead at halftime.

"Hey, let me see the scorebook," Brett said to Brooke as he walked by the bench.

His sister pulled the scorebook back. "You think too much about your stats," she said. "Get the win, then you can see it."

"Come on," Brett said. "I just want to see how I'm doing."

"You're doing fine," Brooke said.

The second half remained tight as the Wildcats and the Panthers played hard. Neither team was able to build much of a lead. With three minutes to go, the score was tied, 38–38.

The Wildcats had the ball. *We need a basket,* Brett thought as he ran downcourt. He spotted Will running down the other side. Brett caught his friend's eye, gave him a quick nod, and the two forwards crossed underneath the basket, trading places on the court.

Garrett passed the ball to Brett on the right wing. Brett faked a shot and drove toward the basket. The Panthers defense angled him away from the basket, so Brett whipped a pass over to Will. Standing in his favorite spot just beyond the three-point arc, Will lofted a long, arching shot. *Swish!*

The Wildcats had grabbed a 41–38 lead.

On defense, Garrett poked the ball away from the Panthers dribbler. Sensing a chance for the Wildcats to score, Brett sprinted back toward the basket. Jeremy, the Wildcats center, grabbed the loose ball.

"Jeremy!" Brett shouted as he ran.

The tall center fired a two-handed overhead pass toward Brett. Taking the bouncing ball in stride, Brett dribbled a couple of times, focused like he did in practice, then laid the ball up against the backboard. It dropped easily into the basket. Just like that, the Wildcats were ahead by five points, 43–38. Another basket by Brett and two free throws by Will sealed the win.

Dripping with sweat, Brett looked up at the scoreboard as the team walked off the court.

"Good game," Will said.

Brett blew out a rush of air. "Yeah," he said. "A little closer than I like 'em."

"The Huskies will be even tougher next week," Will added.

"We can beat them," Brett said.

Coach Giminski was stuffing the basketballs into a large, brown canvas bag. "Good game," he told the boys. "Remember, we've got practice on Wednesday night."

Brett and Will traded one last fist bump as Will started to leave with his father. He looked over his shoulder to Brett and said, "Don't forget my birthday party on Saturday. We're going to Earth Treks."

"What's that?" Brett asked.

"It's a rock climbing center."

"Sounds cool. See you later." Brett walked over to the end of the bench where Brooke was still totaling up the statistics in the team scorebook.

"Well, we got the win." Brett smiled. "Now can I see the scorebook?"

"Okay," Brooke said with a tired look. She spun the book toward Brett.

"What are these?" Brett asked, pointing to the zeroes on the page.

"That's how I keep track of missed shots," Brooke explained.

Brett nodded and made some quick calculations. "Sixteen points," he said. "Not a bad game."

"Not bad at all," Brooke agreed. "You scored almost as many points as the Carlson sisters today."

She closed the book. "If you do as well in the social studies bee, you might get an A on your next report card like me."

The bell for the end of first period sounded and hundreds of sixth, seventh, and eighth graders spilled into the corridors of Einstein Middle School. Brett, Brooke, and Will walked three across down the noisy, crowded corridor. Brooke read questions from a notebook as she walked. "Who was the freed slave who started the abolitionist newspaper called the *North Star?*"

"Frederick Douglass," Will announced, avoiding a group of eighth graders.

Brooke eyed Brett. "Did you know that?"

"Sure," Brett answered.

"Right," Brooke said, as if she didn't

believe him. "You know the rules. One wrong answer and you're out."

"How many kids make the finals in this thing?" Brett asked.

"Four," Brooke answered. "They compete next week."

"The Final Four!" Will grinned.

"This one's for Brett," Brooke said, finding another question. "No help from you, Will. Who did Thomas Jefferson purchase the Louisiana Territory from in 1803?"

"France," Brett said.

"You have to be more specific."

"Um, Napoleon?" Brett said.

Brooke smiled. "Good guess," she said. "You're ready."

"I'd better be." Brett sighed as he turned into social studies class.

Mr. McMillan and Ms. Fromm stood in front of a large room filled with wooden desks. Mr. McMillan was a tall, athletic-looking man with short, dark hair spiked with gel. Ms. Fromm was blonde and just a few inches shorter than Mr. McMillan.

Mr. McMillan held up his hands for

silence. "Everyone, take a seat. Quickly! We have a lot to do today."

The students shuffled into their places as the teacher continued. "As you know, today is the elimination round in the social studies bee on early American history. Four people will advance to the final round." He turned toward the other teacher. "Ms. Fromm will explain the rules. Listen up."

Ms. Fromm stepped forward and read from a single sheet of paper. "The questions will be picked at random by Mr. McMillan and me. If you answer the question incorrectly, you are eliminated and you must return to your seat. The next person in line will then have a chance to answer the question. We will keep asking questions until there are only four students left standing."

Ms. Fromm looked back at Mr. McMillan. "We decide whether an answer is correct. We may ask you to be more specific."

"No instant replay?" Will asked. The class laughed.

"No instant replay," Mr. McMillan repeated. "And another thing: absolutely no help from anyone in the audience. Now let's get started."

The students got up from their desks and went to stand along the walls, bumping into each other and desks along the way. Brett stood next to Will in the middle of the long semicircle.

"Think we're safe here?" Will asked in a low voice.

"No," Brett said.

The teachers moved swiftly through dozens of questions. Lots of kids gave wrong answers and quickly took their seats. Brett stayed standing because he knew Alexander Hamilton was the first treasury secretary and Eli Whitney invented the cotton gin.

When Brett answered that Napoleon sold the Louisiana Territory to the United States in 1803, Brooke gave him a thumbs-up from across the room.

Ms. Fromm flipped through her papers. "What famous American was the only person to sign all three of these documents: the Declaration of Independence, the Treaty of

Paris that ended the American Revolution, and the Constitution?"

Brett had no idea. He looked down the line. *Five kids in front of me,* he thought. *One of them has to know the answer.*

He started to sweat as Ms. Fromm dismissed a series of incorrect answers.

"George Washington?"

"No."

"Thomas Jefferson?"

"Sorry, that's wrong."

"John Hancock?"

"No, I don't believe John Hancock attended the Constitutional Convention."

It was Will's turn next. "Um, could you repeat the question?" he asked weakly.

Come on, Will. Save me, Brett thought as Ms. Fromm repeated the question.

"Ben Franklin?" Will guessed.

"That's right."

Brett let out a sigh of relief. "Clutch answer," he whispered to Will. "Thanks."

"You owe me big-time," Will said.

The questions continued until only five students remained: Brett, Brooke, Will, a girl named Chantelle, and top student in

30

the class Andrew Aaron Anderson. Brett leaned toward Will and whispered, "This is tough competition. Especially with Mr. All-A's. He never gets *anything* wrong."

Brooke and Chantelle started off the final round with a couple of quick correct answers.

The next question was for Mr. All-A's. "What famous museum was started with a gift of half a million dollars from an English chemist named James Smithson?"

"The Smithsonian Institute in Washington, DC," Andrew said without hesitation.

"That's correct."

"The first building opened in 1855," Andrew added. Brett, Will, and Brooke rolled their eyes.

"Gee, we're running out of questions." Ms. Fromm smiled. "You kids have done a terrific job."

Mr. McMillan looked down the list of questions. "Will, you're a sports guy," he said. "What nineteenth-century Hall of Fame baseball pitcher started a sporting goods company that is still in business today?"

Will looked confused. "I don't know," he said. "Somebody named Nike?"

"Sorry, that's incorrect." Mr. McMillan turned to Brett.

"It was Albert Goodwill Spalding," Brett answered.

"We have our four finalists," Mr. McMillan announced as the class cheered.

Will looked at Brett. "How did you know that?" he asked in disbelief.

Brett shrugged. "Lucky guess," he said with a smile.

Will shook his head. "Man, you always win at *everything.*"

Chapter 5

"H ere we are, everybody," Coach Giminski
said as he parked the car in a lot beside
a large warehouse. Brett, Brooke, Will,
and Garrett piled out and walked up to the
entrance. A sign on the door read, "Earth
Treks Climbing Center."

"Let's do it," Will said, throwing open the
door. Brett and the others followed him into
a low-ceilinged room filled with climbing
shoes, athletic clothes, and climbing gear. A
big photo of a man climbing a huge cliff
hung on one of the walls. The man appeared
to be hanging onto the rock with his bare
hands. They walked past a small glass
counter and into the main climbing gym.

"Cool!" Brooke said as they looked all

around. Rock music blared around the gym. The room was like a vast cave, with soaring, rust-colored walls covered with different-colored shapes jutting out like rocks. The walls were not straight, but set at different angles.

"Hey, look at that guy!" Brett said. He pointed at a high climber who was almost upside down on a sharply angled wall. Dozens of blue ropes dangled from the top of the walls to the floor.

"How high are these walls?" Brett asked.

"Something like 50 or 60 feet," Will answered. He elbowed Brett. "Better hang on or..." He pretended to fall back with his hands above his head. "Aaieeeh!"

"Come on, guys," Coach Giminski said. "Quit kidding around. It's very safe. The instructors will show you what to do. They're very good."

Just then, a young man in his twenties approached the group. "Hi, I'm Mike," he said, flashing a friendly smile. "So this is Will's party."

Will's father introduced everyone in the

group. Then Mike clapped his hands and said, "Who's ready to do some climbing?"

As the instructor led everyone to the wall, Brett noticed that the blue floor felt soft and bouncy beneath his sneakers. He listened as Mike explained how the harness and ropes worked and how everything was designed to keep the climber safe. But mostly Brett stared up at the top of the wall, high above him. His mouth was dry and his palms were damp.

"Why don't we start with Will," Mike suggested, "since he's done some climbing before?"

"And he's the birthday boy," Brooke reminded everyone. Will smiled.

Brett watched as his friend, now strapped in a climbing harness, moved slowly and deliberately up the wall. Will placed his feet carefully on the different colored rocks and pushed up. Then he grabbed the plastic rocks above with his bare hands and pulled. By pushing and pulling, Will made his way up the wall like a squirrel inching its way up the trunk of a tree.

Mike held on to the long belaying rope and shouted instructions as Will kept climbing. "Use your whole body. That's it, reach and pull. Make sure you have a good base before you try your next move."

Will was getting smaller and smaller now. When he reached the top, he leaned slightly away from the wall and proudly waved to everyone below. Brooke and Garrett cheered.

"All right!"

"Let's hear it for the birthday boy!"

"Okay, Will, hold on to the rope," Mike said, "and I'll let you down." The instructor worked the belaying rope and Will slid down the wall, bouncing against the rocks with his sneakers every five feet or so. At the bottom, he bounced onto the floor and traded high fives with his dad and his friends.

"Great climb!" Mike exclaimed. "That was real good work."

Will smiled broadly, his face still red from the effort and excitement of the climb. "You should go next," he said to Brett. "It's great."

"Um, okay, but..."

"Come on, it's so cool," Will insisted.

Mike helped Brett into his climbing harness, carefully checking all the hooks and clips on the climbing gear. Together they walked over to the base of the wall.

"Ready to go?" Mike asked.

"Yeah," Brett answered. His throat felt as dry as a desert.

"Just follow the rocks that have the yellow tape under them," Mike said, pointing. "It's like climbing a ladder."

Brett wasn't so sure. He could hardly feel the tips of his hands and feet. He took a deep breath, and started up. Beginning slowly, he moved carefully to each rock, always staying close to the wall. With each move, the floor fell steadily away.

"You're doing great!" Brooke shouted. "You're a regular Spiderman."

A little more than halfway up the wall, Brett looked down and a sudden panic seized him. He grabbed hard at the rocks and pulled himself against the wall.

"Just push off and reach up for the next

rock on the right," Mike called. "You can do it."

Brett started to reach, but he couldn't. His body felt as solid and stiff as the rust-colored wall. His heart was thumping and he was breathing fast and hard. He looked up and down the wall. Mike and the others were calling out instructions and encouragement. But Brett could hardly hear them.

"Just try pushing up one more rock." Mike said. "Like you did before. You can do it."

But Brett still couldn't move. He held onto the rocks with all his strength and tried to re-adjust his feet on the rocks below. His right foot slipped and, in an instant, his grip on the rocks gave way.

He was falling away from the wall!

Suddenly he jerked to a stop and found himself hanging in midair. The harness had tightened around his waist.

"I've got you!" Mike shouted, holding up the rope with both hands. "No problem. You're fine. Just sit back in the harness."

Brett obeyed and Mike lowered him very slowly to the floor like a sack of dirty laundry.

When Brett reached the floor, there were no cheers or high fives. He didn't want to look at anyone. He felt as if he had let all of them down.

Mike clapped him on the back and tried to stay upbeat. "No problem. That happens to a lot of people the first time they climb." He pointed at a blue plastic chair near the base of another wall. "Why don't you go take a break? You can come back and try again later."

Brett went over and sat down, still out of breath.

Brooke followed. "Are you okay?" she asked.

"Yeah," Brett lied.

"Don't sweat it," his sister said. "You got up pretty far." She looked back at the wall. "I better get going. They're waiting for me."

Brett sat in the chair, trying to get the feeling back in his hands and feet. He watched Brooke climb all the way to the top, just like Will. She smiled and waved to him from the top of the wall. Brett gave her a small wave back.

Will came over and sat next to Brett. "Mike wants to know if you want to try again," he said.

Brett watched as Garrett moved steadily up the reddish surface. His heart raced at the memory of clinging so close to the wall and feeling himself slipping. He shook his head. "No, I don't think so."

Will patted Brett on the knee. "Okay," he said, getting up. "We're gonna do a couple more climbs and then go to my house for cake."

"Great." Brett smiled weakly.

His friend walked to the wall, then looked over his shoulder. "Hey, it took a while," he said. "But I think I finally found something I can beat you at."

Brett rested his head against the hard wall. His mind kept going back to when he was stuck on the climbing wall—and worse, when he started to fall. He watched as Will climbed easily again from rock to rock and thought about what his friend had said.

Will was right.

Brett felt totally beaten.

Chapter 6

The ball bounced high off the back rim. Jeremy, the Wildcats center, snatched the rebound out of the air. As soon as his feet hit the floor, he snapped a pass to Garrett.

Coach Giminski jumped off the bench, holding up one finger. "Last shot!" he shouted. "Play for the last shot."

Brett glanced at the scoreboard as he ran downcourt.

WILDCATS   HUSKIES
20   0:20   QTR 2   22

The Wildcats trailed the Huskies by two points, 22–20, with just 20 seconds remaining in the first half. The team had played well, maybe their best game all season, staying close to the undefeated Huskies.

Garrett passed to Brett on the right wing. A Huskies defender pressed close, so Brett quickly passed to Will at the top of the key and then moved to set a pick for his friend.

The Wildcats bench started to count down the final seconds.

"Ten...nine...eight..."

Will looked up at the basket, but he was too far out and too closely guarded for a shot. He drove hard to the basket, trying to move the defender into Brett's pick.

"Seven...six...five..."

It didn't work. The Husky covering Will and Brett moved over to cut off the path to the basket. Without even looking, a desperate Will flipped a pass back over his shoulder to Brett, who was now open.

"Four...three...two..."

Brett caught the ball behind the three-point line. Instantly he pushed a long shot toward the basket.

"*One!*"

The horn sounded while the ball was in the air. Brett's shot bounced off the front rim, the backboard, and the front rim again. Then it dangled in the air for a heartbeat and dropped through the net.

The referee held both hands over his head, signaling a three-point basket. He looked over at the scorer's table. The official at the table signaled with his hand. The basket was good!

The Wildcats were ahead 23–22.

Brett's teammates surrounded him, slapping his back and shouting.

"Sweet shot."

"Buzzer basket!"

"Way to go, Brett."

Will sat down beside Brett. The two boys drank water and caught their breath before the second half. "Great shot," Will said. "We needed that one."

"I was lucky," Brett admitted. "I just threw it up there and it went in."

"We'll need more luck like that in the second half," Will said.

Brett nodded. "Yeah, the Huskies are good. Real good."

Coach Giminski gathered the team for some last-minute instructions. "Same starters as the first half," he said, looking around the huddle. "Keep hustling and looking for good shots. Hands in."

The Wildcats pressed into a tight circle. "One...two...three...defense!" they shouted.

The pace picked up even more in the second half. Every rebound, every loose ball, every possession was a battle. Brett couldn't go anywhere on the court without a Huskies defender's hand in his face or on his jersey.

Despite the Huskies tight defense, Brett kept scoring. A twisting layup, a running right-hander, and a long three-pointer kept the Wildcats close. But Brett's teammates started to cool off and the Huskies began to creep ahead. The Huskies had the ball and a five-point lead, 39–34, with a little more than two minutes to go.

"Come on, defense!" Brett shouted. "We need a stop!"

The Huskies moved the ball patiently, working it around for a wide-open 15-foot jump shot. The ball rattled around the rim and fell off. Jeremy grabbed the rebound and passed the ball quickly to Garrett. The Wildcats point guard looked at the clock and dribbled downcourt. He passed to Brett on the right wing. Brett angled toward the basket but saw Will in the left corner.

We could use a three-pointer right now, he thought. He fired a pass to his friend. The Wildcats forward lofted a shot that found the bottom of the bucket.

Three points! The Wildcats were back in it, 39–37.

The Huskies brought the ball upcourt as the Wildcats applied defensive pressure. Garrett reached around the Huskies point guard and slapped the ball loose, sending it skidding across the floor. Brett dove straight out and grabbed the ball. In an instant, two Huskies wrapped their arms around the ball and Brett.

Tweeeet! The referee blew his whistle and pointed both thumbs straight up to signal a jump ball. Brett looked over to the scorer's table. The possession arrow was pointing in the Wildcats' direction. It was their ball.

"All right!" Brett shouted, pumping his fist. Now they had a chance to tie the score or even take the lead.

The crowd started to make some real noise, with a hundred voices blending into one. Kids started to pound the wooden stands with their feet. Brett could hardly hear himself think.

Garrett dribbled the ball slowly down-court. Brett circled underneath the basket, running the Huskies defender into a pick set by Will. Garrett snapped a quick pass to Brett on the left wing. He caught the ball and saw his chance. In one smooth motion, he spun into the lane, slicing toward the basket. The Huskies center leaped to block the shot. But Brett twisted and lifted the shot over the Huskies center as the two players crashed into each other. Brett saw the ball hit the backboard as he fell to the floor.

The referee's whistle blew as the ball fell through the net.

"And one!" Will shouted.

The referee signaled that the basket was good and Brett would get a foul shot.

Brett looked at the scoreboard as he bounced back up to his feet.

The score was tied, 39–39. And he was going to be shooting for the lead.

Chapter 7

Brett stepped to the foul line as players from the Wildcats and Huskies filled in the spaces along the lane. "One shot," the referee reminded everyone. "The ball's in play."

Brett went through his usual routine before the foul shot. He took a deep breath, spun the ball in his hands, and bounced it three times. Then he spaced his fingertips along the laces of the ball, bent his knees, and sent the ball spinning toward the basket. The ball slid just over the lip of the rim and through the net.

The Wildcats were finally ahead again, 40–39.

The Huskies called time out. The Wild-cats jumped off the bench, pounding Brett on the back for his clutch free throw. Even though he was grinning from ear to ear, Brett brushed his teammates aside. "Come on. The game's not over," he said as every-one gathered around their coach.

"Listen up," Coach Giminski said.

Brett concentrated hard so he could hear the coach's instructions over the crowd's cheers and the kids' pounding feet.

"Forty-five seconds left," the coach said, looking up at the clock. "Remember, play tough defense. Keep moving your feet. Try not to foul. Make them take a tough shot."

Brett and Will exchanged glances in the huddle. This was just the kind of game they always dreamed about playing when they were shooting baskets in the park. The score was close, the other team was tough, and the gym was noisy.

After the time-out, the Huskies moved the ball around, looking for the go-ahead basket. The Huskies star forward curled into the lane for a running, right-handed shot. The Wildcats defense reacted, but they were a split second too late. The Huskies shot bounced around the rim and fell in.

The Wildcats were behind again, 41–40.

"Time-out," Garrett signaled after taking a few quick dribbles downcourt.

The Wildcats crowded around Coach Giminski. He grabbed a clipboard with a basketball court outlined in black on its white surface. Brett and the other Wildcats stared at the board as he diagrammed a play.

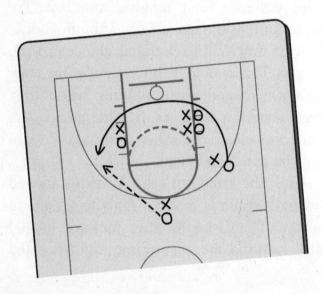

"Garrett, you bring the ball down," the coach said, his blue marker moving furiously over the clipboard. "Brett, start on the right wing. Fake as if you're looking for a pass and then cut under the basket. Will and Jeremy, help Brett get open on the right side of the lane." He pointed the marker at Garrett. "Get Brett the ball on the left side." He looked straight at Brett. "It's up to you. If you have a shot, take it or try to drive to the basket. If you're covered, look for Will in the corner."

"Which corner?" Brett asked.

"Left."

Brett nodded. The referee blew his whistle. Coach Giminski looked around the huddle. "Everybody got it?" he asked. Now all the Wildcats nodded. "Okay, let's go!"

The Wildcats ran the play just as their coach had drawn it on the clipboard. Garrett passed the ball to Brett the moment he popped open on the left wing. Brett turned to face the basket. The Huskies defense was coming on fast. Brett decided he wasn't open enough for a jump shot so he drove hard to the right, hoping to get a shot off in the lane. But a Huskies defender cut him off. Then he remembered what Coach Giminski had said: *Look for Will in the corner.* Brett could see Will standing open at the left edge of the court, his favorite spot. Brett swung a hook pass over his head. Will caught the ball in the corner and flipped up a quick jump shot. The ball looked good in the air. But this time, it bounced high off the back rim and away from the basket. The Huskies grabbed the rebound. Brett looked at the clock as he ran upcourt.

Fifteen seconds left, he thought. *Down by one.*

The Huskies brought the ball upcourt, passing the ball away from the Wildcats in a crazy game of keep-away.

"Foul him, foul him!" Coach Giminski screamed from the bench, frantically waving his arms over his head. But his voice was swallowed up in all the noise swirling inside the gym.

Brett raced to defend the Wildcats basket. *Can't let them score an easy bucket,* he told himself. The Huskies spread out around the floor as their bench started to count down the final seconds.

"Ten...nine..."

The Huskies had the ball along the right sideline near half-court. Will and Garrett charged toward it. Brett spied one of the Huskies wide open on the right with his hands outstretched, calling for the ball.

"Eight...seven..."

Sensing a chance to make a play, Brett sprinted toward the open player. Sure enough, at almost the same instant, the unsuspecting Huskies forward let go a cross-court pass. Running at full speed, Brett stretched out his right hand and tipped the ball toward the unguarded basket.

"Six...five..."

He grabbed the spinning ball, several steps ahead of the surprised Husky. Now, the countdown of the final seconds was drowned out in a wave of thunderous sound.

But inside Brett's head, there was an eerie quiet. As he dribbled to the basket, he repeated Coach Giminski's familiar instructions from their layup drills: *Take it up strong. Aim for the top right corner of the square on the backboard. Easiest shot in basketball.*

Just as Brett pushed off the floor, he felt a sudden stiffening of his right elbow, like the panic he had felt when he was pressed against the climbing wall at Will's birthday party. The ball went up just a little low and to the right of the square on the backboard. It danced on the rim, curled around the lip of the iron, and fell off the hoop. The ball hit the floor as the buzzer sounded.

The game was over. The Wildcats had lost. Brett had missed the easiest shot in basketball.

Chapter 8

Brett could hardly remember anything that happened after the missed layup. He lined up with the rest of the team to shake hands with the Huskies, but he was moving in a daze. The sounds and words around him were muffled and confused. He almost felt like crying. But he couldn't start bawling in front of Will and all his team-mates.

Coach Giminski patted Brett on the shoulder as Brett was gathering his basket-ball stuff. "Don't worry about it. You played a good game," he said. "We'll get another chance. We play the Huskies again in a couple weeks."

Brett nodded without saying a word.

Will said, "Good game. See you around."

The car ride home was quiet too. Brett stared out the back window. When he closed his eyes, he could still see the ball going up to the basket and bouncing around the rim. But every time, even in his daydream, the ball fell away. Every time he still missed.

Brett's dad broke the silence. "It was a really good game," he said. "Both teams played very well."

"The Huskies are good," Brett's mom agreed.

Brooke looked at him across the backseat. She didn't say anything. Brett knew his twin sister understood that he didn't feel like talking about the game or anything else.

Mrs. Carter tried to change the subject. "So when are the big finals of the social studies bee?" she asked.

"Tuesday morning," Brooke answered.

Mr. Carter forced a smile. "Hey, I bet it's not very often a family has two kids in the running," he said. "I guess we have a fifty-fifty chance of winning."

"I wouldn't be so sure," Brooke said. "All-A's—Andrew Aaron Anderson—is pretty tough."

Mrs. Carter turned around. "Hey, can parents come to watch the finals?" she asked.

"No!" Brooke practically shouted.

"Why not?" Brett's mother asked. "I'm sure Mr. McMillan and Ms. Fromm wouldn't mind since you're both in the finals."

"Parents don't come to school," Brooke said firmly.

"They do on Back-to-School night," Mr. Carter said.

"That's different," Brooke said. "Everyone is invited on Back-to-School night." She folded her arms. "You guys *can't* show up. And that's final," she said.

Brett's father looked in the rearview mirror. "What do you think, Brett?" he asked. "Should your mom and I come watch you guys?"

"You don't want to go," Brett said in a flat

voice. He looked out of the window again. "I'll probably miss a question like...Who was the first president of the United States?"

"Come on now," his dad said, still looking in the mirror. "It wasn't that bad."

"It was pretty bad," Brett said. His voice was shaky.

"You made a great play, stealing the ball," Mr. Carter said.

"You were just a little unlucky at the end," Brett's mother added.

Brett knew that wasn't true. It hadn't been bad luck. He had been nervous. He had been scared, just like on the climbing wall.

"I lost the game," he said.

"If it hadn't been for you," his father pointed out, "your team would have lost by 20 points."

Brett shook his head. "I lost the game," he repeated.

His parents glanced at each other. There was no more talk about the bee or basketball or anything else for the rest of the ride home.

The house was dark when they pulled into the driveway. Brett's mom clicked on the lights as they walked in the front door. Jumper was instantly at their feet, wagging his tail and looking for someone to play with.

"See, Jumper still loves you," Brooke said to her brother. She leaned down to scratch behind the dog's ears.

"I'll check our messages," Brett's mom said, heading down the hall to the phone.

"Any calls?" Brett's dad asked when she came back.

"Just Grandma."

"What did she want?"

Mrs. Carter looked a bit embarrassed. "She wanted to know how Brett's game went."

Brett threw his sports bag into the corner of the laundry room. "I'm gonna take a shower," he said and ran upstairs.

After his shower Brett sat on the edge of his bed, dressed in jeans and a Los Angeles Lakers T-shirt. He rubbed a towel into his wet hair. There was a knock at the door. "Come in," he said, without looking up.

Brooke stepped into the room. "Hey, you never looked at the scorebook," she said. "Do you want to see it?"

Brett shrugged. "I guess so."

Brooke sat down next to him and opened the scorebook.

"Eighteen points, seven rebounds," Brett's sister said. "You even had a couple of assists. That's a pretty good game. If it weren't for you, you guys would have lost by 20 points."

"Yeah," Brett said. He was staring at the last empty circle in his scoring line in the fourth quarter. The missed layup.

He slammed his wet towel against the bed. "The easiest shot in basketball," he muttered. "I've made a million of them."

Brooke closed the scorebook and headed for the door. "Don't worry. You play the Huskies at the end of the season. You'll get another chance." Then she added, "And hey, maybe you'll win the social studies bee. Of course, you'll have to beat me first."

Yeah, Brett thought. *And All-A's.* He got up and crossed the room to where the Wildcats schedule was taped on the wall. Taking a pen from his desk, he wrote in the final score.

RISING STARS LEAGUE—BIG EAST CONFERENCE

Date	Opponent	Time	
Dec. 13	Panthers	1 p.m.	W 41-36
Dec. 20	Golden Eagles	2 p.m.	W 50-26
Jan. 10	Orangemen	4 p.m.	W 38-29
Jan. 17	Cardinals	noon	W 49-40
Jan. 24	Panthers	3 p.m.	W 47-38
Jan. 31	Huskies	2 p.m.	L 41-40
Feb. 7	Orangemen	1 p.m.	
Feb. 14	Golden Eagles	4 p.m.	
Feb. 21	Cardinals	noon	
Feb. 28	Huskies	1 p.m.	

"Easiest shot in basketball," Brett muttered to himself.

Chapter 9

Brett and Brooke moved swiftly through the halls of Einstein Middle School. They each held a long list of American history questions in their hand.

"Who was the Union general at the Battle of Gettysburg?" Brooke asked.

"General Meade," Brett said. "You already asked me that."

"Okay," Brooke said. "You ask me a question, then."

"Where was the agreement signed that ended the Civil War?" Brett stepped around a kid stuffing things in his locker.

"At Appomattox Courthouse," Brooke replied. "Which two generals signed the agreement?"

"That's easy, Grant and Lee." Brett smiled, thinking he might trip Brooke up with the next question. "What did General Grant allow the Confederate soldiers to keep after they surrendered?"

Brooke gave her brother a strange, questioning look. "That wasn't on the list."

"So what?" Brett shrugged. "I'll bet All-A's will know it."

Brooke paused outside the door of their social studies class as the others students filed into the room. Finally she shook her head. "I don't know. Their uniforms?" she guessed.

Brett shook his head. Then he spied All-A's standing at the front of the class. "Hey, Andrew!" he called.

The boy turned around. "Yeah?"

Brett repeated the question.

"Their horses," Andrew replied. He turned away, not even waiting for Brett's response.

"Is that the answer?" Brooke asked.

"Yep," Brett replied.

"Figures," Brooke said, shaking her head.

She and Brett walked into class and sat next to Will.

Will elbowed Brett. "Final Four, baby," he said. "Big game today." He held a pen up to his mouth like a microphone and continued speaking as if he were a sports announcer. "This is what it's all about. Today is for"—he paused dramatically—"the World Social Studies Championship."

"So are you betting on me to win?" Brett asked.

"No, he's betting on *me*," Brooke said.

Will looked at them as if they were both crazy. "Are you kidding?" he asked. "I figure All-A's will take it without even trying." He smiled and jerked a thumb at Brett. "Anyway, I figure this guy will choke again."

"What's that supposed to mean?" Brett snapped.

"Maybe you'll blow an easy layup question," Will teased.

Brett glared at his friend. "Maybe if you'd made that shot from the corner—"

Will held up his hands. "Hey, I'm just kidding," he said. "When did you get to be Mr.

Super-Sensitive? You always give *me* a hard time."

"Quiet," Brooke warned them. "Here they come."

Mr. McMillan and Ms. Fromm walked into the suddenly quiet classroom. "Okay, everybody, let's get started," Mr. McMillan said. "You know the rules. Let's have the four finalists up here."

Brett, Brooke, All-A's, and Chantelle got up from their desks and stood in front of the room.

"Those of you who aren't in the finals, pay attention," Ms. Fromm told the class. "Lots of these questions will be on Friday's unit test."

All the students let out a low groan.

"Okay, Brooke," Mr. McMillan began. "First question…"

The finalists sailed through the first rounds. Brett didn't choke. He got all the easy "layup" questions. He knew that the first ten amendments to the Constitution were called the Bill of Rights. He knew that Meriwether Lewis and William Clark led the first American expedition into the Louisiana Purchase.

After Ms. Fromm took over, the questions got harder. Still, all four finalists hung tough. Finally Ms. Fromm asked Brett, "Who was the only delegate from New York at the Constitutional Convention to sign the Constitution?"

Brett felt a trail of nervous sweat trickle down his back. This was the first time that day a question had stumped him. Standing beside him, All-A's rocked back and forth as if he couldn't wait to push Brett aside and blurt out the answer.

"Could you repeat the question?" Brett asked, stalling for time.

Ms. Fromm repeated it. But still nothing came to Brett's mind.

"DeWitt Clinton?" Brett guessed. He saw Will fall back and groan at his seat.

"No, I'm sorry. That's wrong," Ms. Fromm said.

"Andrew?"

"Alexander Hamilton." The answer practically burst out of the boy's mouth.

"Alexander Hamilton is correct."

Brett moved slowly back to his seat. He traded a slight fist bump with Will.

"Hey, no worries," Will said, slapping him on the back. "You did okay."

Brett said nothing but moved around in his chair, unable to get comfortable. He was disappointed to be the first finalist to get eliminated. But mostly he was still mad at Will for bringing up the missed layup.

He turned his attention back to the bee. Chantelle, Andrew, and Brooke battled through three more rounds of questions. Then Chantelle missed one. "What was the first major battle of the American Civil War?"

"The Battle of Bull Run!" All-A's practically shouted when it was his turn.

Now it was up to Brooke. If she didn't get her question right, then All-A's would be the winner.

Will leaned over to Brett. "Man, it's like All-A's wrote the textbook," he whispered. "Brooke doesn't stand a chance."

Brett frowned. "Come on, Brooke," he called out. "You can do it."

Mr. McMillan looked up. "No cheering," he warned. "Even from a twin brother."

But Brooke couldn't beat All-A's. She forgot that General George Washington's army spent the winter of 1777 in Valley Forge, Pennsylvania.

All-A's gave the answer right away, even though he didn't have to. He'd already won.

"I guess we're both losers now," Brett said as Brooke sat down.

"What are you talking about?" Brooke said, looking annoyed. "I came in second out of the whole class. I only missed one question. That doesn't make me a loser." Then she added, "And by the way, in case you didn't notice...I beat you."

She was right about that. Brett slumped back in his chair.

First, the wall.

Then the missed layup.

And now this...

Brett shook his head. *Nothing* was going right anymore.

Are you ready?" Brooke asked, poking her head in Brett's room. Brett sat at his desk chair in his Wildcats uniform. He had one basketball shoe on. The other was in his hand.

"Yeah," he answered. But he still didn't move.

"Better get going," Brooke said. "We're leaving in five minutes."

She turned to go, then turned back, her hand still on the doorknob. "Are you okay?" she asked. "You're usually ready way before a game."

"I'm okay," Brett said. He bent over to tie his shoes. "I just don't want to mess up again."

He could already feel the butterflies fluttering around in his stomach. In the past, he'd always been excited before a game and ready to play. Today was different. Now he was scared.

"You're not still thinking about that stupid layup, are you?" Brooke asked.

Brett didn't answer. He didn't have to.

"Forget it," Brooke said with a wave. "Everybody misses shots. Even me. And Will misses plenty. I keep the scorebook, remember? Come on, let's go."

Brett took a deep breath and tightened his laces. "Ready."

An hour later, he stood at midcourt with his hands on his hips, watching Will shoot free throws. He looked up at the scoreboard.

The Wildcats led the Orangemen by two points, 28–26, with a little more than five minutes to go in the game. It had been an ugly game with long stretches when neither team could buy a basket. Brett had struggled too. Instead of driving to the basket, he was settling for shooting jump shots. A few of the longer shots had fallen in, but most bounced off the rim. Brett could almost feel Brooke writing down a zero in the scorebook every time he missed.

At the foul line, Will dipped and shot. The ball hit the front rim and fell away.

"Come on, Will, still got one more!" Brett shouted, clapping his hands at midcourt. "A little higher."

Will seemed to take Brett's advice. The second shot was higher and swished through the net. The Wildcats led 29–26.

On the next trip upcourt, the Orangemen point guard faked a shot and drove to the basket. He tossed a running right-hander that rattled around the rim and went in. The Wildcats lead was now only one point, 29–28.

Clinging to their slim lead, the Wildcats started being extra careful. No player seemed to want to take the next shot. Finally Brett tossed up a 15-foot jump shot from the wing. The ball bounced away from the basket and the Orangemen center snagged the rebound.

"Time out," called the Orangemen coach. He was fired up now and so were his players. The Orangemen were clapping and shouting. The Wildcats bench was much quieter, with only Coach Giminski doing the talking.

"Listen up. We're still ahead by one point, but there's plenty of time left." He drew up a new defensive formation on his clipboard.

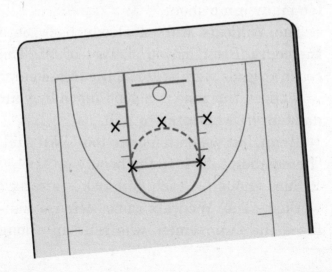

"Let's surprise them," he said, pointing to the defense. "Let's switch from playing man-to-man defense to a 2-3 zone. Don't let them get close to the basket. Force them to take the outside shot." The coach tossed the clipboard back on the bench. "When we get the ball, keep passing it around," he went on. "But let's drive to the basket and either score or get fouled."

The team nodded.

"Brett!" Coach Giminski said sharply.

Brett's head popped up. The coach was looking right at him. "Take the ball to the basket," he ordered. "You've been shooting too many jump shots."

The Wildcats walked slowly back onto the court. Brett moved slowest of all. The coach's words were still ringing in his ears.

"I think the zone is a good move by your dad," Brett whispered to Will.

"Yeah, but we better score too," Will said. "Remember, take it to the hoop."

Sure enough, Coach Giminski's strategy worked. The Wildcats zone defense confused the Orangemen, who sent up a long shot from the corner that missed. Will grabbed the rebound and the Wildcats hustled downcourt, looking to add to their one-point lead.

Garrett passed the ball to Brett on the right wing. The Wildcats forward faked a shot and drove toward the basket. *I don't want to blow another layup,* Brett thought as he got closer to the basket. He quickly tossed a pass to Will at the corner. Will flipped a pass to Jeremy, who was standing closer to the basket. The big Wildcats center sent up a sweeping hook shoot that rolled around the rim and fell in the bucket.

Now the Wildcats were ahead 31–28. "Great shot, Jeremy!" Brett shouted as he ran back on defense.

Coach Giminski was on his feet and waving his arms. "Stay in your 2-3 zone!" he called. He held up two fingers on one hand and three fingers on the other.

The Wildcats zone worked again. After a few passes, the Orangemen shot another desperate three-pointer from deep in the corner. Will snatched the rebound and was fouled immediately. The referee signaled that Will would be shooting one-and-one.

Brett stood bent over at half-court, tugging at the edge of his basketball shorts. He glanced at the clock. Twelve seconds left.

"Come on, Will, make one," he whispered. He didn't want the game to come down to one last shot like the Huskies disaster.

Will took a deep breath and spun the first foul shot to the basket.

Swish!

"All right!" Brett shouted. The Wildcats were now safely ahead by four points, 32–28.

Will missed the second shot, but it didn't matter. The final buzzer sounded just as the Orangemen scored on a last-second layup.

The Wildcats had won 32–30.

After the teams shook hands, Brett walked over to his sister on the bench. "You want to see the stats?" she asked, looking up from the scorebook.

"I'm not sure I do," Brett said with a tired grin.

Brooke turned the book toward him.

"I didn't help much today," Brett replied.

"You did some good things." Brooke shrugged. "You got a few rebounds and played decent defense. And you guys won. That's the important thing."

"I missed a lot of shots," Brett said, eyeing the long list of zeroes in his line.

Brooke closed the scorebook with a snap. "Coach Giminski's right," she said. "You've got to drive to the basket."

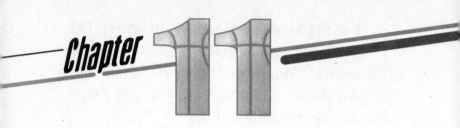

Chapter 11

T hree!" Garrett shouted out as the ball dropped through the net. Brett moved up one spot in the rebounding line. The Wildcats were practicing their layups again, trying to get to twenty in a row.

"Four," Jeremy called as another shot fell through.

Coach Giminski stood to the side, giving his team a steady stream of instructions. "Take it up strong. Easiest shot in basketball. We've got to make our layups if we want to keep winning."

The Wildcats were still on a winning streak, but just barely. Last Sunday, they'd defeated the worst team in the league, the winless Golden Eagles, 38–25. Brett had played his worst game of the season. He'd missed most of his shots, including a couple more layups, bounced the ball off his feet a few times, and played like someone who couldn't wait for the game to end.

The layup count kept going up as each shot went through the hoop.

Brett could feel the pressure mounting inside him as he moved through the shooting line and closer to his turn. He bounced on his feet like a fighter in a boxing ring, trying to get some feeling back in his toes.

"Nine..."

Now it was his turn. He grabbed the bounce pass, took two quick dribbles, and pushed off his left foot.

Brett felt his whole body stiffen as he leaped toward the rim. He could sense that he wasn't shooting the ball as much as he was trying to guide it into the basket. The ball didn't quite reach the upper right corner of the square on the backboard. It bounced along the right edge of the rim just like in the Huskies game. But this time the ball caught the front lip of the rim and fell through.

"Ten!" Brett shouted louder than any of his teammates. He ran quickly to the end of the rebounding line.

The count continued to climb higher. "Eleven...twelve...thirteen...fourteen..." Brett calculated that he would be the player in line to shoot the crucial twentieth layup.

"Keep it going!" Coach Giminski shouted. "Remember, guys, we get to twenty or no scrimmage."

But Brett didn't want the Wildcats to keep it going. *Come on, somebody miss,* he thought, clenching his teeth.

The shots kept falling and the count went higher.

"Fifteen...sixteen...seventeen..."

No one had missed so far. Brett started to take deep breaths, trying to slow down his racing heart. *Easiest shot in basketball,* he reminded himself.

"Nineteen..."

Will skipped a waist-high bounce pass to Brett, who bobbled it for a split second and then recovered. He took one strong dribble and laid the ball up against the top right corner of the square marked on the backboard. But it was too hard. The ball bounced off the front rim and away from the basket.

"Oh no!" all the Wildcats groaned.

Brett stood for a few seconds near the side of the basket with his hands on his hips, staring up at the rafters. *I can't believe I blew another layup,* he thought.

"Start it over," Coach Giminski insisted. "I want twenty." He stood on the sidelines with his arms crossed tightly against his chest. His eyes followed Brett as if he were studying him.

Almost ten minutes later, after more misses by Brett and several of his teammates, the Wildcats finally reached twenty.

"Okay, hurry up," Coach Giminski said, blowing his whistle. "We only have a few minutes left to scrimmage. Same teams as last practice."

Brett and Will stood at midcourt. As always, they were on opposite teams in the scrimmage and covering each other.

"That took forever," Will said.

"Yeah," Brett said.

"We would have been scrimmaging a long time ago," Will started, "if—"

"If what?" Brett cut him off angrily.

Will looked straight at Brett. "If *you* hadn't missed that twentieth layup," he said.

Brett was mad but he didn't say anything. He knew his friend was right.

The pace of the scrimmage was fast and furious. When Brett got the ball, Will was right on top of him, daring him to drive to the basket. Brett swung the ball around, trying to get some space. But Will didn't budge an inch and Brett passed the ball to Garrett.

"When he comes up on you like that, Brett, drive to the basket," Coach Giminski called from the sidelines. The coach glanced at his watch. "Next basket wins."

Brett lofted a long shot that bounced off the rim. Jeremy snapped down the rebound and passed it upcourt to Will. Brett raced to cover his buddy. But Will would not be denied. He dribbled hard to the basket, with Brett hanging on his left. Will jumped toward the basket, holding the ball high in his right hand and away from Brett.

Going for the block, Brett reached across Will's body with his left hand. But he couldn't reach the ball. Will flicked a shot against the backboard and through the net.

"Yes!" Will cried, pulling down a fistful of air.

A few minutes later, Brett sat on the gym floor, staring blankly at Brooke's basketball practice. He barely noticed his sister and her teammates practicing their jump shots.

Basketball wasn't as much fun anymore. Ever since he had frozen on the climbing wall at Will's birthday party, ever since he had missed the layup in the Huskies game, he had been scared. Scared of letting everyone down. Scared of missing an easy shot. Scared of being the goat.

Coach Giminski threw the brown equipment bag over his shoulder and walked up to Brett. Will was a step or two behind his father.

"You've just got to take it to the basket,

Brett," Coach Giminski reminded him again. "You should always be looking for a layup."

"Okay, Coach," Brett said without even looking at him.

Coach Giminski stood over Brett for a long moment, as if he were still studying him. Finally he said, "There's one more thing I want you to do."

"Practice my layups?" Brett asked with a tired smile.

"No," Coach Giminski said, shaking his head. "What are you doing this Saturday morning?"

Chapter 12

Brett sat in the Giminskis' minivan and stared out the window. He held his breath for a count of three and then let it out slowly. It was Saturday morning and he was on his way to the Earth Treks climbing wall again.

Why did I let Coach talk me into this? Brett thought. *I'm probably gonna choke again.*

Will's dad filled the car with basketball talk as he drove. "Listen, Brett, I know you think you lost the Huskies games by missing that layup," he said. "But you guys both know, teams win games and teams lose games."

Will looked back from the front passenger seat. "Yeah," he agreed. "If I had hit my shot from the corner, we wouldn't have needed your layup."

Brett knew that Will and his dad were trying to be nice. But he wasn't having any of it.

"We had a chance to beat the Huskies," he said. He pressed his hands down on the seat, trying to control his anger. "And I blew the easiest shot in basketball."

"That happens sometimes," Coach Giminski said. "But you made the right play. You took it right to the basket. It just rolled off."

Brett still wasn't convinced. "I choked," he said simply. "I was the goat."

"Other players have choked worse than that," Coach Giminski said as he turned a corner.

"Yeah, like who?" Brett asked.

"Well, there was an NCAA men's basketball game back in the 1990s," Coach Giminski began. "It was a great game between Michigan and North Carolina. Michigan had a terrific team with five guys who had started together as freshmen."

"Freshmen?" Brett blurted out, suddenly interested. "Five of them? No way."

"They called them the Fab Five," Coach Giminski said. "You know how everybody wears baggy basketball shorts now?"

"Yeah."

"The Fab Five started that."

"You're kidding," Will said.

"No, I'm not. Anyway, Michigan's best player was a guy named Chris Webber," Coach Giminski continued. "The game was real close and Michigan got the ball in the last few seconds. They had a chance to take a final shot to win the game."

He paused as he waited for the light to turn green. "But then Chris Webber called time out," he said.

"What's wrong with that?" Brett asked, confused. "He was giving his team a chance to set up a play."

"Problem was, Michigan didn't have any time-outs left," the coach said. "In fact, the Michigan coach had reminded the team that they had no time-outs left during its last time-out."

"So why...?" Brett started to ask.

"I guess in all the excitement, he just forgot," Coach Giminski said.

"What happened?" Will asked.

"It's a technical foul to call a time-out when you don't have one," Coach Giminski explained. "North Carolina shot a free throw and got the ball. That clinched the championship for the Tarheels."

Brett's head fell back on the backseat as he tried to imagine how Chris Webber must have felt. "Wow, the NCAA championship, on national TV. He must have felt terrible to blow it like that."

"He probably did, for a while," Coach Giminski agreed. "He turned pro some time after the game."

"Was he any good?" Brett asked.

"Sure, he was an NBA All-Star for a couple of years," Coach Giminski said. "He never won a championship, but he kept playing and had a nice career."

The coach was waiting at another light,

but Brett could tell he was thinking about old basketball games.

"Then there was Fred Brown," Coach Giminski went on.

"Who'd he play for?" Will asked.

"Georgetown. Back in the 1980s, when they had Patrick Ewing."

"Hey, Ewing was really good," Brett said, perking up. "My dad talks about him all the time."

"He was *really* good," Coach Giminski said. "Anyway, Georgetown was playing North Carolina for the NCAA championship in 1982. North Carolina had just taken a one-point lead on a basket by Michael Jordan."

"*The* Michael Jordan?" Brett asked. He leaned forward.

"Yup." Coach Giminski nodded. "He was a freshman. So anyway, Fred Brown was Georgetown's point guard and he was bringing the ball downcourt as time was running out—"

"He didn't call a time-out he didn't have, did he?" Will interrupted.

Coach Giminski chuckled. "No. But he

looked to his left and then passed to a guy who was all alone to his right."

Brett was confused again. "So what's wrong with that?" he asked.

"The guy he passed to was from North Carolina," Coach Giminski explained. "He dribbled upcourt and ran out the clock."

"Oh man," Brett groaned. His head sank back onto the seat again.

"Fred Brown's coach must have killed him," Will said.

Coach Giminski shook his head as he steered the car into the Earth Treks parking lot. "Not at all," he said. "The Georgetown coach was named John Thompson. He gave Fred Brown a big hug and told him not to worry about it. Said that he had helped the team win lots of games and that he was sure he'd help them win some more."

"What happened to Fred Brown after that?" Brett asked.

Coach Giminski put the van in park and turned around in his seat. "Two years later, Georgetown was back in the championship game against the University of Houston," he said. "This time, Georgetown won. And you know who was the first player Coach Thompson hugged?"

"Fred Brown?" Brett asked.

"That's right," Coach Giminski said. "You see, he didn't let one bad pass, one mistake, get him down. He kept playing and he came back."

Brett, Will, and Coach unbuckled their seat belts and got out of the van. Coach Giminski clapped his hand on Brett's shoulder. "Okay," he said. "Let's start *your* comeback. Right now."

Chapter 13

Everything at the climbing center looked the same as before: the low-ceilinged room filled with climbing gear, the climbing pictures on the wall, the cavelike main room with its rust-colored walls that reached up...*way* up.

Brett's feelings were the same too: the sweaty palms, the dry mouth, the jumpy feeling in his entire body like he couldn't stand still. *What have I gotten myself into?* he thought as they walked into the main climbing room.

"There's Mike," Coach Giminski said.

Mike came over, dressed in black shorts and a white T-shirt with the words "Freedom to Roam" in big red letters across the front. "How are you guys doing today?" he asked. Then he looked at Brett. "Hey, aren't you the guy who had some trouble on the wall a couple of weeks ago?" he asked.

"Yeah, I'm the one," Brett said, looking away.

"Don't worry about it," Mike said with a wave. "Like I said, it happens all the time. I'm glad you decided to come back." He looked around the room. "Why don't we get started?"

The group walked over to the climbing wall.

"Do you want to go first?" Mike asked. "Or do you want to watch Will first?"

Brett looked at Will and his dad. "No, that's okay," he said. "I'll go up first."

Mike helped Brett into his climbing harness, snapping the buckles and clicking all the metal clips in place. Once again he explained how the ropes worked.

Finally he asked, "Are you ready?"

Brett nodded quickly, without saying a word.

Mike smiled. "Still nervous, huh?"

"Yeah," Brett admitted.

"Well, there's nothing wrong with that," Mike assured him. "Happens to everybody. Even me, when I make a new climb. Being a little nervous is a good thing. It makes you more careful." Then the instructor clapped Brett on the back and said, "Okay, let's go."

Here goes nothing, Brett thought. Then he started up, staying close to the wall. He reached up, grabbed the rocks, and pulled while pushing off the rocks with his feet. From his last climb, Brett knew the first 10 or 15 feet would be easy. The trouble would come later, somewhere in the middle of the wall.

Brett had only gone a few feet when Mike shouted, "Stop right there, Brett!"

What did I do wrong? Brett wondered. He held on tight and pressed himself closer to the rocks. He could feel his heart pounding against the rust-colored wall.

"Do you have a good, solid stance?" Mike asked.

Brett felt his hands and his feet. "Yeah," he answered.

"Okay, I want you to keep your grip and that stance," Mike said in a calm voice. "And then move your body...slowly...away from the wall."

Brett checked his hands and feet again. Following Mike's instructions, he eased back so that his chest was no longer pressed against the wall.

"See how your hands and feet can keep you on the rock?" Mike called. "You don't have to stay right up against the wall. Give yourself a little more room. That way you can move more easily on the surface."

Brett nodded. He carefully moved away from the wall and began to feel more comfortable, less pinned down. *Maybe I can do this,* he thought.

"Okay, now keep climbing," Mike said.

Brett took a deep breath and started inching up the wall.

Mike kept shouting instructions and encouragement from below. "That's it. Now reach out with your right hand. You're doing great. Remember, you don't have to be so close to the wall. Use your whole body."

By now, Brett was more than halfway up the wall and beginning to sweat. Instinctively he moved closer to the wall again.

"Why don't you take a quick break right there?" Mike said. "Move away from the rock a bit and take a couple of good, deep breaths."

Brett did what he was told. He took a series of deep breaths while staring straight into the wall. He didn't dare look down. Instead, he looked up and saw he had around 15 feet or so—maybe a dozen more moves—left to the top. His legs and arms felt heavy. *How can I do this?* he wondered.

Then Mike's voice came from below again. "Just take it one move at a time. Nice and slow. You don't have to go until you're ready."

Without looking either down or too far up, Brett started his ascent again. He reached and pulled with his right hand. Then he pushed off with his left foot. He set a new grip with his left hand, pushed off with his right foot, and reached with the left hand. *Don't get too close to the wall,* he reminded himself. *Check your feet, take a deep breath, and then reach up with your right hand.*

By now, Brett was almost to the top. His heart racing, he pushed off with his right foot and reached with his left hand. He felt for the smooth top edge of the wall with his fingertips.

"I did it!" Brett shouted the moment his finger touched the top. He could hear Will and Coach Giminski cheering.

"All right!"

"Way to go, Brett."

"You made it to the top."

Mike took charge above all the cheering. "Great work, Brett. Now sit back in the harness and I'll bring you down."

Brett felt a huge rush of relief when his feet touched the spongy surface of the floor underneath the wall. He looked at Mike, who was helping him out of the harness.

"It wasn't the greatest climb," Brett said. "I took forever."

"Hey, don't beat yourself up," Mike said.

"You made it. You want to go up again?"

"Uh...maybe some other day," Brett answered quickly. He'd definitely had enough for now.

Will and his father came over as Brett was stepping out of his harness. Both of them were smiling from ear to ear. Coach Giminski clapped Brett on the shoulder. "I think pretty soon this guy will be ready to take on the Huskies," he declared.

"First we've got to play the Cardinals," Will reminded his father.

Coach Giminski's smile got even bigger. "Brett is definitely ready for the Cardinals."

Chapter 14

Brett took a crosscourt pass from Will. He was about 15 feet from the basket with a Cardinals defender draped all over him. He still went up for the jump shot. The ball felt good as it left his hand, but it bounced off the rim.

Another miss, Brett thought as he ran back on defense.

Coach Giminski jumped off the bench. "Take it to the hoop, Brett!" he shouted. Then he snapped his fingers and signaled for another Wildcats player to go in.

The whistle blew after the Cardinals scored another basket. Ellis walked onto the court, tapped his chest, and pointed at Brett. "I'm in for you, Brett," he called.

Brett took a seat on the far end of the bench. He looked up at the scoreboard.

WILDCATS   CARDINALS
15   2:00 QTR 2   21

The Wildcats trailed the Cardinals 21–15 with two minutes left in the first half. Brett took a long drink of water and wiped his face with a towel. "Come on, let's go!" he shouted to his teammates, slapping the towel against the hardwood floor.

Coach Giminski walked over and squatted in front of Brett like a baseball catcher. "Listen, when the defense is playing up on you like that, you've got to drive to the basket," he said sternly. But then he softened his tone. "You can do it," he told Brett. "You climbed the wall yesterday, didn't you?"

Brett nodded. He knew the coach was right. He was still playing scared, shying away from the basket, afraid of blowing an easy shot. He sat on the bench, watching the Wildcats and the Cardinals score a couple of baskets apiece before the end of the first half. But mostly he was trying to gather his courage, just as he had done on the rock wall. He knew he needed to try to climb past his fears again.

At halftime, Will joined Brett on the bench. "We gotta come back," he said, out of breath. "If we lose this one, we've got no chance to catch the Huskies."

"Don't worry," Brett said, staring straight ahead. "We'll come back."

Will glanced at Brett. "All right," he said with approval. "Sounds like you're ready."

"Set me a few picks," Brett said. "I'll do the rest."

At the beginning of the second half, Garrett passed the ball to Brett on the left wing. Once again the Cardinals defense was on him tight, clinging to him like a damp shirt. Will moved over to set a pick to Brett's right. Brett faked left and drove right, sending his man crunching into Will's pick. Brett tossed a running right-hand shot over the leaping Cardinals center. The ball bounced around the rim and fell off.

"Arrgh!" Brett shouted in frustration as he watched the Cardinals grab the rebound.

But Coach Giminski was excited. "Good move!" he shouted from the sidelines. "Keep taking it to the basket."

The next time down the court, Brett got the ball in the same spot and faked right as if he were going to use Will's pick again. The Cardinals defense reacted. But this time Brett crossed over his dribble and drove left, angling to the basket. Just as he was about to try a left-handed layup, the Cardinals center leaped to block the shot. Brett slipped the ball into his right hand, slid underneath the basket, and spun a shot off the backboard.

"Yes!" he shouted as the ball splashed through the net. He flew back up the court to play defense.

Brett's twisting layup sparked a Wildcats comeback. The team started scrapping for loose balls, playing harder defense and hitting more shots. Brett made some shots and missed some others. But at least he was playing more like his old self. He was taking the ball to the basket and not just settling for long shots. Finally a jump shot by Will pulled the Wildcats into the lead, 44–42.

The Cardinals coach jumped up after Will's basket. "Time-out!" he cried, forming his hands into the letter *T*.

Everyone on the Wildcats bench was on their feet and making noise.

"Great shot, Will."

"Way to hustle!"

"That's how we take it to the hoop, Brett."

Kneeling on one knee in front of the bench, Coach Giminski tried to settle his excited team. "Listen up," he said. "Three minutes to go. We're only up by two." He looked down the Wildcats bench and said, "They're getting tired. Let's try to run when we get the ball, okay? Get some easy baskets."

The Cardinals' first shot was a miss. Jeremy grabbed the rebound and snapped a pass to Garrett.

"Let's go!" Garrett shouted, following Coach Giminski's orders to run. He dribbled fast up the middle, with Will racing up the left and Brett racing up the right. The Wildcats' fast break caught the Cardinals by surprise, and they had left only one player back on defense. Garrett drove straight to the basket, faked left, and then dished a pass to the right. The play happened so fast that Brett didn't have time to think or get nervous. He caught the pass and, in one smooth motion, laid the ball against the backboard. It dropped straight into the hoop!

Brett beamed as he raced upcourt. "Great pass!" he shouted, pointing at Garrett.

The Cardinals kept missing and the Wildcats kept running. They scored three more fast-break baskets to win the game 52–42!

The whole teamed stormed the court, cheering and yelling.

"Great second half, Brett," Will blurted out as he threw his arm around Brett. "You were playing like the old Brett, the one I could never beat."

"I missed some shots," Brett said above the cheers as they jogged off the court with the team. "Even in the second half."

"Like my dad says, everybody misses shots," Will said. "You made plenty today."

"Thanks, but I'd better make some more if we want to beat the Huskies," Brett answered. He grabbed a towel off the bench and wiped his face, then waved at his mom and dad in the crowd. They were cheering and smiling. He walked over to the scorer's table and didn't have to say a word to his sister. Brooke flipped the scorebook around so he could study the game's stats.

"I was a lot better in the second half than the first half," he said.

"Not bad," Brooke said, nodding. "Hey, you're getting there. At least you started going to the hoop." She smiled and added, "You may even finally be ready for the Huskies."

Chapter 15

'm open!" Brett called out. His sister passed him the ball on the right wing. Will charged out to stop his shot. Brett spun on the playground blacktop and drove past Will to the basket.

Garrett moved over to defend. Brett thought for a split second of passing to Brooke. Instead, he tossed a slightly off-balance shot against the metal backboard. The shot was too high and too hard and bounced away.

Garrett grabbed the rebound and flipped a pass to Will beyond the three-point line.

"Take Will," Brett told Brooke. "I've got Garrett."

Brooke took her defensive stance in front of Will, who tossed a quick pass toward Garrett. Brett lunged forward, but missed the pass by a fingernail. Garrett took two quick dribbles and put the ball in.

"Ten to ten!" Will shouted. "Tie game."

Brett smacked his hands together in frustration. "If I had made that shot, we would have won."

"Forget the shot," Brooke scolded him. "Just play defense. You've got Will." She looked at Will and Garrett. "Gotta win by two baskets, right?"

Garrett shook his head. "Nope. Next basket wins," he said. "I'm already late for my piano lesson." He passed to Will, who drove to the basket. Brett was right with him, angling him away from the basket. Will threw a running right-hander up over Brett's outstretched arm. The ball rattled off the backboard and through the metal chain net with a *clink*.

"Yes!" Will yelled. "I win again."

Brett groaned. "Lucky shot," he said.

"Hey, it went in." Will smiled.

Garrett grabbed his basketball from the sideline. "Gotta go," he said. "See you guys Sunday at the Huskies game."

Brett flipped the ball against the backboard and through the net. Then he passed the ball to Brooke. "We should have won," he said.

"Don't sweat it," Brooke said as she swished a ten-foot jump shot. "I should have made more of my shots."

Without saying a word, Brett, Brooke, and Will started to move around the blacktop, taking shots, making passes, grabbing rebounds.

"Better save your shots for the Huskies game," Will said to Brett after he swished another long jumper.

"What's their record?" Brooke asked, passing the ball to Brett.

"Eight and one, just like us," Brett said, banking in another shot. "The winner on Sunday wins the league championship." He sent up another jump shot. "I hope I don't blow it like I did in the first game," he said.

"You've been playing a lot better lately,"

Brooke said, snagging a rebound.

Brett shrugged.

"Look, I know," Brooke insisted. "I keep the stats. What are you worried about?"

Will looked around the park. The sun was sinking fast. It hovered in the late winter sky just above a row of distant trees. "What do you guys want to play now?" he asked. "Two against one?"

"Nah. We can't make fair teams," Brett said. "How about H-O-R-S-E?"

"That takes too long," Brooke said, eyeing the setting sun.

"I know." Will brightened. "Let's play Twenty-One."

"Two points for a foul shot and one point for a layup, right?" Brett asked.

"Yeah, that's it," Will said. "And it's foul shot, layup, foul shot, layup."

"No wonder you want to play that," Brett said. "Half the shots are layups. You know I stink at those."

"You've been making some today," Brooke pointed out.

"Yeah, and I've been missing some too," Brett said.

"Come on, it's getting dark," Will said, dribbling the ball to the foul line. "I'll go first."

"I'm second," Brooke called.

"Guess that means I'm last," Brett said.

"Remember, you've got to make a foul shot before you can shoot your first layup," Will said. "After that, if you miss a foul shot, you can take one more layup, but only one. Then your turn is over, whether you make the layup or not."

He bounced the ball and spread his feet at the foul line. Then he dipped and shot. The ball rattled around and fell in. Will grabbed the ball and tossed in a layup. "Three points," he said.

The next foul shot bounced off the rim. Brooke grabbed the rebound and held the ball. "Do you get one more layup?" she asked.

Will held out his hands for the ball. "Yeah," he explained. He made the layup. "Okay, now it's 4–0–0," he said.

Brooke made two foul shots and three layups. "That's 4–7–0," she called out after her turn.

Brett stood on the foul line and went through his foul-shooting routine.

Deep breath.

Spin the ball.

Bounce the ball three times.

Place your fingertips on just the right spots.

Dip and shoot.

The basket was good!

Brett grabbed the ball and went in for the layup. The shot felt too hard, but the ball bounced around the loose metal rim and finally fell through. He dribbled back to the foul line.

"Almost, buddy, almost," Will teased.

"It went in," Brett said.

After the first layup, Brett found his rhythm. Foul shot. Layup. Foul shot. Layup. He could feel his confidence growing with every shot. "That's nine," he declared.

Another foul shot.

Another layup.

"That's twelve."

There was no doubt about the next few shots. Each found the bottom of the bucket, barely disturbing the metal net.

"Fifteen...eighteen."

"One more foul shot and one more layup and I win," Brett said. He bounced the ball three times and then sent the ball spinning toward the rim.

Swish!

Will held the ball for a moment. "Don't blow the layup now."

"Just give me the ball," Brett said.

His friend bounced a pass to Brett's waist, just like in practice. Brett took a quick dribble and pushed off toward the basket. The ball felt good leaving Brett's hand, but it somehow spun around the rim and out.

"Aaargh!" Brett cried, bending over at the waist as if he were in pain. "I don't believe it."

"Don't worry," Brooke assured him. "Just be sure to make it against the Huskies."

Chapter 16

Brett stood in front of his bedroom mirror doing a final check of his uniform. He wore a clean white T-shirt underneath his basketball jersey. He tucked both shirts into his shorts, but not too tightly. He wanted to be able to move easily around the court. Then he leaned over and pushed his athletic socks down around the tops of his high-top sneakers.

"You ready?" Brooke asked, standing at the door.

"I guess so," Brett said. He eyed his sister and added, "I still feel kind of nervous."

"Look, you're supposed to feel nervous before a big game," Brooke said. "And this is a big game."

Brett shook his hands to loosen his arms and shoulders. "Yeah, but am I supposed to be *this* nervous?" he said.

"Hey, what's the worst that can happen?" Brooke asked.

"I can mess up again," Brett said.

Brooke laughed. "You already messed up. And you survived. You're still playing, aren't you?"

"Yeah, I guess you're right," Brett said.

When they arrived at the gymnasium, it was crowded and noisy. Almost every seat on the bleachers was taken. Mr. and Mrs. Carter had trouble finding seats and ended up in the top corner of the stands.

Coach Giminski called his team together. "As you know, the Huskies are a really good team," he reminded the Wildcats. "We've got to play hard the whole game." He looked around the circle of players. "If we win today, we win the championship."

Brett stood near the edge of the huddle, bouncing on the balls of his feet.

"You okay?" Will asked.

"I'm okay," Brett said, still bouncing.

Minutes later the Huskies jumped off to a quick 6–2 lead, hitting their first three shots before the Wildcats could make a basket.

Brett missed his first shot, a long jumper from the corner.

"Take it to the basket!" Coach Giminski reminded him.

Brooke's right, Brett thought as he raced toward the action. *I can't mess up any worse than last time. I just have to play.*

On the next possession, Garrett passed the ball to Brett at his favorite spot on the right wing. This time Brett faked a shot and drove hard to the basket.

The referee's whistle blew just as Brett tossed up his shot. The ball bounced off the backboard and straight through the strings. "The basket is good," the referee shouted as he signaled with his hands. "Foul on Number Five. One shot."

Brett went through his usual foul-shot routine, spinning the ball and bouncing it three times. *Just like when we played at the park,* he told himself as he shot the foul shot.

Swish. The score was 6–5. The Wildcats were back in it!

The game and the lead bounced back and forth. The Huskies surged out in front on a couple of three-pointers. But Brett and the Wildcats kept coming back. Brett scored a few more baskets, including a couple of driving, twisting layups to tie the score at halftime, 25–25.

For the first time in a while, Brett was hustling and taking it hard to the hoop. But his improved play was not enough. In the fourth quarter, a three-pointer by a Huskies guard gave the Huskies a 39–34 lead.

"Come on, guys, we need a basket!" Garrett shouted to his teammates as he dribbled the ball downcourt. The Wildcats passed the ball around, looking for a good shot. Brett got the ball on the wing and looked up. The Huskies defender was right there. Brett lowered the ball and his shoulder and took a quick step as if he were going to drive straight to the basket. The Huskies defender stepped back to block the hoop.

Brett's fake had worked. Now that he had more room, he flipped up a quick jump shot to the basket. *Swish!* Brett checked the scoreboard as he raced upcourt.

WILDCATS 36 3:35 QTR 4 HUSKIES 39

Now the Wildcats were down by three with just a few minutes remaining. They had to dig in on defense and stop the Huskies. Brett's legs felt heavy and sweat dripped off his face. He was way past tired, but he kept his feet moving on defense. When a Husky tried to pass the ball to his teammate on the left, Brett flicked his hand and tipped the ball into the open court. The Husky dove out to get the ball, but Brett tapped it farther into the open court. The two of them scrambled for the ball, but Brett outpaced his opponent and got it easily.

Brett's mind flashed back to the earlier

118

Huskies game, but he didn't hesitate. He dribbled hard to the basket. As he went up for the layup, he felt his arms go tight and got a nervous flutter in his chest. But he laid the ball against the backboard and—it went into the hoop!

Now the Wildcats were only down by one, 39–38.

"Great play, Brett!" his coach shouted. "That's how we take it to the basket."

"Easiest shot in basketball," Will said, slapping Brett's raised hand.

Brett laughed. "Not for me."

The Wildcats and Huskies traded baskets as time wound down. A spinning layup by Brett put the Wildcats ahead 46–45 with just 30 seconds to go.

The Huskies called time out.

Coach Giminski knelt in front of the Wildcats bench and gave his instructions in a calm voice. "Thirty seconds to go, guys. We're up by one. Try not to foul. Just move your feet and play good defense." Then he added, "We don't have any time-outs left. So we can't call a time-out if we get the ball."

Brett looked at Will and nodded. He didn't want to be another Chris Webber.

When the teams returned to the court, the gym swelled with sound. Cheers for both teams bounced off the walls and rose to the ceiling.

The Wildcats defense hung tough, never giving the Huskies an unguarded look at the hoop. With ten seconds to go, both benches started the final countdown.

"Ten...nine..."

Desperate, a Huskies forward leaned back and tossed up an off-balance jump shot.

Swish! The Huskies were ahead 47–46.

"Eight...seven..."

Jeremy passed the ball inbound to Garrett, who started dribbling downcourt.

"Six...five..."

Garrett passed to Brett near midcourt.

Get to the basket, Brett thought. He started to his right, did a quick crossover dribble, and powered his way up the middle of the court.

"Four...three..."

Brett looked up, hoping to see Will in his favorite spot in the left corner. But the Huskies had his buddy covered.

"Two..."

Brett dribbled fast, but he was still 20 feet from the basket. *Not enough time for a layup,* he thought, *I gotta shoot...now!* He pushed off his left foot and let go a running right-hand shot. The ball was straight in line with the basket.

"One!"

The buzzer went off as the ball sailed through the air. Brett landed near the foul line just as the ball hit against the back of the rim and bounced straight back toward him. He caught the ball with both hands as the Huskies started their wild celebration around him.

The Wildcats—and Brett—had lost. Again.

Chapter 17

Brett moved down the line with the rest of his teammates, slapping weak high fives with the victorious Huskies.

"Good game."

"Good game."

"Good game."

When every hand was slapped, the Huskies began to celebrate their championship win by pointing into the air and shouting, "We're Number One!"

The Wildcats walked slowly back to their bench. Some of the players sat down and stretched out their legs and stared across the floor. The season was over. The team seemed to linger more than usual, as if by staying on the gym floor they could make the season last a little longer.

Brett stood near the scorer's table with his hands on his hips and a towel draped around his shoulders.

"You want to see the book?" Brooke asked.

Brett shook his head and rubbed the towel through his sweat-soaked hair.

"You had a real good game," Brooke said, turning the book and nudging it closer to Brett. "Maybe your best of the season."

"I know how I did," Brett said. He gazed back at the Huskies, who were still celebrating as they gathered their basketball bags. "We still lost."

Brooke shrugged and spun the book back toward her. "Have it your way," she said.

Coach Giminski circled his hands above his head to gather the team around him. "Listen up," he said. "You guys had a good season. Make that a *great* season. You came really close to winning it all."

Standing with his teammates tight beside him, Brett flinched a little at Coach

Giminski's words: *Really close.* He closed his eyes as the coach kept talking. He could almost see the layup in the first Huskies game rolling off the rim.

"Everybody played hard. And you guys played as a team. I'm real proud of that," Coach Giminski went on. "And everybody improved as the year went along. So I want you to keep playing and I hope to see everybody back next season." He turned and started to put the basketballs into his brown canvas bag.

The Wildcats started to drift away. Brett sat down on the bench.

"Good game," Jeremy said, reaching down to slap Brett's palm as he passed. "You played great."

"Thanks," Brett said. "You too. See you next season."

"See you down at the park," Garrett said. The boys traded a silent fist bump as Garrett walked on.

Brett's parents came out of the stands and stood by the bench as the rest of the crowd filed out of the gym.

"That was a great game," Mr. Carter said as he shook hands with Coach Giminski. "Thanks for a terrific season."

"That last shot was *so* close, honey," Mrs. Carter added to Brett. She looked like she was holding herself back from reaching down to the bench and hugging her son.

"Brett made the right play," Coach Giminski said, nodding. "He took it right to the basket. He was going for a layup and he just ran out of time. He took a good shot. It just didn't go in."

Brett leaned against the row of bleachers behind him. "I was so sure it would," he said. "I thought we were going to win."

"Thought you were going to be Fred Brown?" Coach Giminski smiled. "And win the championship when you got a second chance?"

"Yeah," Brett said, remembering the story. "I thought I was going to be like Fred Brown."

"It doesn't always turn out that way." Coach Giminski shrugged. "Maybe next season." He tossed the bag of basketballs over his shoulder. "But the important thing is that you came back. You played. And you played well."

The group was quiet for a moment. "I can't believe the season is over," Will said as he looked around the almost-empty gym.

"Yeah, what are we going to do next weekend without any basketball games?" Brett said.

"Hey, I know! Want to go to Earth Treks on Saturday?" Will asked. He looked at Brett and Brooke. "Rock climbing will help us stay in shape for sports."

"Sure," Brooke said.

Will looked straight at Brett. "What about you?" he asked. "Want to come?"

Brett glanced up at the high, hard wall in back of the basket. He remembered how he had felt when he froze on the climbing wall that first time. Then he thought back to the layup that he had missed in the first Huskies game.

But then he remembered his second climb at Earth Treks and how it had felt to touch the flat surface on the top of the wall.

And he thought about this last Huskies game and how his hustle and twisting layups had fueled the comeback that had fallen just inches short.

"Sure," Brett said. "Count me in."

The Real Story

The Michigan Wolverines played the North Carolina Tarheels in the 1993 NCAA men's basketball championship game. Each team had been seeded number one in its bracket. Basketball fans all over the country could hardly wait to see the big game.

Michigan was led by five players, known as "the Fab Five," who had all started as freshmen. The best player among the Fab Five was Chris Webber, an All-American 6-foot, 10-inch forward who was a terrific scorer, rebounder, and passer.

The Wolverines and Tarheels battled deep into the second half, locked in a tight, hard-fought game. Michigan had the ball with only a few seconds left. They trailed North Carolina by a score of 73–71 but had one more chance to take a final shot to tie the game or maybe win the game on a three-pointer.

Chris Webber got the ball along the sidelines near the Michigan bench. He was covered closely by two Tarheels, and with time running out, he couldn't find an open teammate. Desperate, Webber frantically signaled a time-out.

Michigan, however, did not have any time-outs left. In fact, the Michigan coach had reminded his team, during its previous time-out, that they had none remaining. In the excitement of the final seconds, however, Chris Webber had forgotten his coach's warning.

The referees called a technical foul against Michigan for calling a time-out when it didn't have one. With 11 seconds to go, North Carolina shot free throws and got the ball. Michigan didn't have a chance. Webber's mistake helped clinch the national championship...for North Carolina.

Webber, however, did not let his mistake in the biggest college game of the year keep him from being a good basketball player. He turned pro shortly after the North Carolina game. Webber played for several teams during his fifteen-year career in the National Basketball Association (NBA). He was the NBA Rookie of the Year in 1994 and was named to the NBA All-Star team five times. Now Webber is a basketball commentator for ESPN. He has been active in various charities including his Timeout Foundation. The foundation's mission is to provide positive educational and recreational opportunities to youth.

Fred Brown was another basketball player who didn't let one mistake ruin his basketball career. The Georgetown Hoyas played the North Carolina Tarheels in the 1982 NCAA men's basketball championship game. The game was another back-and-forth contest. With just 17 seconds left on the clock, the Tarheels took the lead, 63–62, on a basket by a freshman named Michael Jordan. That is the same Michael Jordan who later won ten NBA scoring titles and six NBA championships with the Chicago Bulls.

Fred Brown, the Georgetown point guard, brought the ball downcourt after Jordan's basket. Time was running out, but Georgetown hoped to hold on to the ball and take one last shot to win the game. Brown looked to his left and then passed to someone he thought was an open teammate on his right. The "teammate" was James Worthy, a star forward for North Carolina. Worthy dribbled away the final seconds, clinching the victory for the Tarheels.

After the game, the Georgetown coach, John Thompson, hugged Brown and told him not to worry about his mistake. He said he told his heartbroken point guard that he had helped Georgetown win lots of games. And he had a feeling that Brown, who was then just a sophomore, would help them win more in the future.

Coach Thompson was right. Fred Brown kept playing and was an important part of the Georgetown teams that finished with a record 22 wins and 10 losses in 1983 and 34 wins and just 3 losses in 1984. That year, Georgetown was back in the championship game against the University of Houston. This time, Georgetown won the NCAA Championship 84–75. And the first player Coach Thompson hugged after the game was senior guard Fred Brown.

In sports, even the best players can make mistakes that cost their team a big game. But they can't give up. Just like Brett, or Chris Webber or Fred Brown, they have to keep playing and try to make a comeback.

The author thanks Mike Lyons, the head climbing team coach at the Earth Treks Climbing Centers in Maryland, for his help with the climbing scenes in the book. He also thanks Nadia Abouraya for her help in typing the original manuscript.

About the Author

Fred Bowen was a Little Leaguer who loved to read. Now he is the author of many action-packed books of sports fiction. He has also written a weekly sports column for kids in *The Washington Post* since 2000.

For thirteen years, Fred coached kids' baseball and basketball teams. Some of his stories spring directly from his coaching experience and his sports-happy childhood in Massachusetts.

Fred holds a degree in history from the University of Pennsylvania and a law degree from George Washington University. He was a lawyer for many years before retiring to become a full-time children's author. Bowen has been a guest author at schools and conferences across the country, as well as the Smithsonian Institute in Washington, DC, and The Baseball Hall of Fame.

Fred lives in Silver Spring, Maryland, with his wife Peggy Jackson. Their son is a college baseball coach and their daughter is a college student.

Be sure to check out the author's websites.
www.fredbowen.com
www.SportsStorySeries.com

Become a fan of Fred Bowen on Facebook!

Hey, sports fans!

Don't miss all the action-packed books by Fred Bowen.
Check out www.SportsStorySeries.com for more info.

Fred Bowen Sports Story series

Want more?

All-Star Sports Story Series

T. J.'s Secret Pitch
PB: $5.95 / 978-1-56145-504-1 / 1-56145-504-0

T. J.'s pitches just don't pack the power they need to strike out the batters, but the story of 1940s baseball hero Rip Sewell and his legendary eephus pitch may help him find a solution.

The Golden Glove
PB: $5.95 / 978-1-56145-505-8 / 1-56145-505-9

Without his lucky glove, Jamie doesn't believe in his ability to lead his baseball team to victory, until he learns that faith in oneself is the most important equipment for any game.

The Kid Coach
PB: $5.95 / 978-1-56145-506-5 / 1-56145-506-7

Scott and his teammates can't find an adult to coach their team, so they must find a leader among themselves.

Playoff Dreams
PB: $5.95 / 978-1-56145-507-2 / 1-56145-507-5

Brendan is one of the best players in the league, but no matter how hard he tries, he can't make his team win.

Winners Take All
PB: $5.95 / 978-1-56145-512-6 / 1-56145-512-1

Kyle makes a poor decision to cheat in a big game. Someone discovers the truth and threatens to reveal it. What can Kyle do now?

Want more?

All-St★r Sports Story Series

Full Court Fever
PB: $5.95 / 978-1-56145-508-9 / 1-56145-508-3

The Falcons have the skill but not the height to win their games. Will the full-court zone press be the solution to their problem?

Off the Rim
PB: $5.95 / 978-1-56145-509-6 / 1-56145-509-1

Hoping to be more than a benchwarmer, Chris learns that defense is just as important as offense.

The Final Cut
PB: $5.95 / 978-1-56145-510-2 / 1-56145-510-5

Four friends realize that they may not all make the team and that the tryouts are a test—not only of their athletic skills, but of their friendship as well.

On the Line
PB: $5.95 / 978-1-56145-511-9 / 1-56145-511-3

Marcus is the highest scorer and the best rebounder, but he's not so great at free throws—until the school custodian helps him overcome his fear of failure.